Amazing Rhymes

Edited By Kelly Reeves

First published in Great Britain in 2020 by:

Young Writers
Remus House
Coltsfoot Drive
Peterborough
PE2 9BF
Telephone: 01733 890066
Website: www.youngwriters.co.uk

Printed and bound in the UK by BookPrintingUK
Website: www.bookprintinguk.com
YB0444O

FOREWORD

Here at Young Writers our defining aim is to promote the joys of reading and writing to children and young adults and we are committed to nurturing the creative talents of the next generation. By allowing them to see their own work in print we believe their confidence and love of creative writing will grow.

Out Of This World is our latest fantastic competition, specifically designed to encourage the writing skills of primary school children through the medium of poetry. From the high quality of entries received, it is clear that it really captured the imagination of all involved.

We are proud to present the resulting collection of poems that we are sure will amuse and inspire.

An absorbing insight into the imagination and thoughts of the young, we hope you will agree that this fantastic anthology is one to delight the whole family again and again.

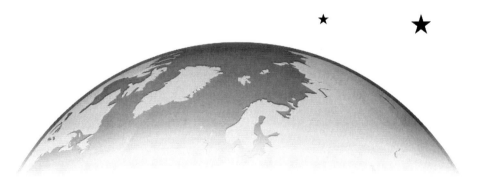

CONTENTS

Appleton Wiske CP School, Appleton Wiske

Birdwell Primary School, Birdwell

Buckingham Park CE Primary School, Buckingham Park

Halstow Primary School, Greenwich

Molly Norris (7) 57
Amelie Yates (8) 58
Eira Perilioglu (8) 59
Liam Hermreck (7) 60

Hartlebury CE Primary School, Hartlebury

Joyce-Joan Staines (8) 61
Demetri Withers (8) 62
Emma Riches (9) 63
Eleanor Webber (8) 64
Freja Palmer (9) 65
Martha Plant (8) 66
Olivia Steele (8) 67
Alexander Summers (9) 68
Oliver Haydon (9) 69
Syd Cole (9) 70
Scarlett Terry (8) 71
Ella Mulcahy (9) 72

Knightwood Primary School, Chandlers Ford

Yixiang Hou (9) 73
Sai Mistry (10) 74
Devraj Landa (9) 75
Eloise Davies (9) 76
Abigail Flood (10) 77
Megan Lewis (9) 78
Millie Rickerd (9) 79
Matthew Talboys (10) 80
Eva Thompson (10) 81
Ben Humphrey (9) 82
Charlotte Green (10) 83
Benjamin Wasenczuk (9) 84
Jake Bray (10) 85
Esme Cole (10) 86
George Edwards (10) 87

Llwyncrwn Primary School, Beddau

Kieran Brown (11) 88

Tia-Leigh Norman (10) 89
George Stewart-Durose (10) 90
Ethan Ollis (9) 91
Issabel Lawry (10) 92
Jayden Baker (10) 93
Lailamai Evans (10) 94
Robert Norfolk (10) 95
Amy Algren-Carter (10) 96
Darcey Morgan (10) 98
Jayden Fisher (11) 100
Aimee Hearse (10) 101
Keeley Webb (10) 102
Charlie Reeves (11) 103
Ben Gilley (10) 104
Ethan Freeman-Jones (11) 105
Isabelle Shearer (10) 106
Georgia Thomas (10) 107

Manston Primary School, Crossgates

Oliver Jones (10) 108
Emma Maloney (10) 109
Lily Banks (9) 110
Dominic Carlos Azevedo (9) 111
Katie Froggatt (9) 112
Jack Kilcoyne (10) 113
Freddie Laycock (10) 114
Zac Brennan (10) 115
Archie Charles Partner (9) 116
Avaneesh Gupta (9) 117
Grace Hooks-Sellers (10) 118
Summer Orme (10) 119
Isla Wishart (9) 120
Michael Azevedo (9) 121
Scarlett Guilfoyle (10) 122

Paddox Primary School, Rugby

Hubert Cybulski 123

Pennyhill Primary School, West Bromwich

Tammie Carlmain (11)	124
Sachroop Atwal (9)	125
Kelly-Ann Spoors (8)	126
Molly Troth (8)	127
Maryam Khan (11)	128
Nancy Chidera Ozoemena Ugochukwu (9)	129
Ellie-Mai Bernice Gibson	130
Anointed Reginald (10)	131
Jaiden Jassi (8)	132
Jayden Burns (10)	133
Amanpreet Kaur (10)	134
Marcell Samuels (11)	135
Iisha Egan (9)	136
Kirat Singh (9)	137

Pheasey Park Farm Primary School, Great Barr

Inayah Jeffers (9)	138
Leila-Rose Ferguson (9)	139
Heidi Hunter (9)	140
Kyle Ball (9)	141
Ella Greenhill (9)	142
Liam Hegney (9)	144
Olly Bryant (9)	145
Eli Richards (10)	146
Isabelle Forrester (10)	147
Corban Sargent (9)	148
Henry Deavall (10)	149
Lara Aziz (10)	150
Niamh Brayson (9)	151
Rohan Child (9)	152
Sabrina Alizadah (10)	153
Hollie Venner (10)	154
Carrie Davis (9)	155
Lilly Hunt (10)	156
Layla Babbington (10)	157
Kodie Webb (9)	158
Liam Durrant (10)	159
Ella Horsley (10)	160

Sydney Davis (9)	161
Ruby Mya Francis (9)	162
Alfie Gardner (10)	163
Ethan Wood (9)	164
Amelia Baingana (10)	165
Dexter Leathem (9)	166
Alexander Williams (9)	167
Jacob Bryant (10)	168
Haillie Hobson (9)	169
Jack Lloyd-Roberts (9)	170
Daisy Hollyoake (9)	171
Lacey Pritchard (10)	172
Malachi Jagirdar (10)	173
Lilly-May Jordan (9)	174
Lucy Allan (9)	175

Sherburn Hungate Community Primary School, Sherburn In Elmet

Joshua James Hobson (10)	176
Mary Herridge (10)	177
Holly Elizabeth Hodcroft (9)	178
Vanessa Subaciute (9)	179

St James CE Primary School, Birmingham

Arjun Sond (10)	180
Maria Malhi (10)	182
Monet Wright (10)	184
Alimah Begum (8)	185

Sunnylands Primary School, Carrickfergus

Anamika Ullas Nair (10)	186

Tollcross Primary School, Edinburgh

Eliza Smeed (9)	187
Martha Crawford (9)	188
Abdulaziz Softa (9)	189
Finn Laidler (9)	190

George Ewing (9)	191
Matias Edwin Gonzalez (9)	192
Sam McCartan (9)	193
Aaron Hedley (9)	194
Rayyan Shafique (9)	195
Kiayla Curry (9)	196
Rubi Keles (8)	197
Maria Vilaro-Rojas (10)	198
Georgio Adesanya (9)	199
Essa Lahoak (9)	200
Steven Mccoag (9)	201
Marc Armada (9)	202
Scarlet Macdonald (9)	203
Dean McMenigall (10)	204
Harris Gray (9)	205

Two Rivers Primary School, Amington

William Gallivan (11)	206
Elisha Wale (11)	207
Nate Ray (10)	208
Archie Castagna (10)	209

THE POEMS

My Alien Zachary

Z ooming, zappy Zachary,
A liens up high,
C harging round the universe,
H igher than the sky,
A mazing, accurate flier,
R ough but isn't a spier,
Y oghurt-loving friend, who loves going round bends.

T ough but weak,
H e loves to shriek,
E ating chocolate bars.

A way he goes to Mars
L aughing funny actor
I diotic brain
E ats rocks and tractors
N aughty but tame.

Daniel Thomas James Green (10)
Appleton Wiske CP School, Appleton Wiske

Adventure In Space!

I am a soft feather,
Drifting over the moon,
As I hear crunch, crunch, crunch,
It's an astronaut tune!

Just a bit like me,
Aliens are funky!
As we party all night,
We are all monkeys!

I feel lighter than dust,
And luckier than you!
We just must, must, must,
It's a space restaurant.

Beepety! Blopety! Boo!
Guess what I can hear?
Big, boisterous footsteps, but who?
Just a mystery for me and you...

Isla Grainger (11)
Appleton Wiske CP School, Appleton Wiske

Flying Saucers

In the blink of children's eyes,
There are flying saucers in the skies,
You can hear the twinkling stars,
When they fly around Mars.

Magical, magnificent, mysterious,
Always very serious,
Red, yellow and green,
It is very big for a machine.

Sparkling, shimmering, spotty moon,
The flying saucer lands whilst he sings a tune,
Bang, crash, rumble!
The flying saucer needs some apple crumble.

Melony Gibson (10)
Appleton Wiske CP School, Appleton Wiske

My Meteorite

M y zooming, zapping meteorite

E ats gooey, buggy mites

T he meteorite is like a ball of cheese,

E asily zooms like a breeze,

O ff it goes to red, rosy Mars

R ough, raggedy and round, he likes chocolate bars

I t is a flying, hard cricket ball

T he meteorite is just so tall

E ven though he doesn't have a friend, he's never alone.

Kayden Michael Andrew Hodgson (10)

Appleton Wiske CP School, Appleton Wiske

Jelly Telly Alien

Alien jelly
Watches telly
Squash squeeze
Always sneeze
Gruesome, gross
Never close
Pork pies
Attack dies
Outer space
Scary face
Slimy bed
Mouldy bread
Cheesy moons
Planet balloons
Googly eyes
Secret spies
Lazy legs
Yucky eggs.

Katie Hutchinson (9)
Appleton Wiske CP School, Appleton Wiske

Saturn

S pace is part of the galaxy

A stronauts walk through the air

T ea and water look like bubbles floating

U p in the blackness, all with the planets

R ound and round the rocket ship goes

N ew planet nobody knows!

Riley William Michael Jackson (10)

Appleton Wiske CP School, Appleton Wiske

All About Space

S paceship soaring up to space like a firework
P lanets are as colourful as a rainbow
A stronauts spacewalk on the moon
C elestial stars glow far away
E xciting spaceships looking for planets.

William King (10)

Appleton Wiske CP School, Appleton Wiske

The Christmasalisaurs

A kennings poem

Planet-stomper
Water-freezer
Snowflake-chomper
Nose-sneezer
Dice-cheater
Wing-glider
Snow-eater
Friend-hider
Big-brother
Hug-lover
Blue-blaster.

Sophie Connolly (9)

Appleton Wiske CP School, Appleton Wiske

Yorkshire Man

A kennings poem

A flat cap wearer
A parkin eater
A pudding pumpkin lover
A tea drinker
A whippet walker
A terrier taker
A kestrel flyer
A lamp miner
A pipe poker
A white rose lover
A God's own county
A greenery seeker
A ferret liker
A tweed wearer
A silent talker

I'm proud to be a Yorkshire man!

Maggie Rose Randall (9)
Birdwell Primary School, Birdwell

Yorkshire Man

A kennings poem

A flat cap gatherer
A white rose taker
A terrier walker
A pudding eater
A parkin lover
A ferret keeper
A tweed wearer
A whippet follower
A sand stealer
A tea drinker
A silent speaker
A kestrel flyer
A pipe smoker
A green wearer
A ferret walker
A parkin maker
A white rose lover.

Callum Jubb (8)
Birdwell Primary School, Birdwell

Yorkshire Man

A kennings poem

Whippet walker
Parkin patriot maker
Pudding patriot lover
Pipe smoker
Kestrel comber
Terrier taker
Flat cap wearer
White rose wearer
Tea taker
Ferret keeper
Tweed wearer
Field lover
Silent stalker
Seaside stumbler

I'm glad to live in God's own country.

Poppy (8)
Birdwell Primary School, Birdwell

Yorkshire Man

A kennings poem

Aye'up, I'm a flat cap wearer
A whippet walker
A kestrel flyer
A brilliant batter
A pudding eater
A silent talker
A pipe smoker
A parkin eater
A white rose wearer
A tea drinker
A tweed wearer
A green wearer
A nature wanderer

I am a proud Yorkshire man.

Ollie Browning (9)
Birdwell Primary School, Birdwell

Yorkshire Man

A kennings poem

A tweed wearer
A whippet walker
A kestrel flyer
A flat cap wearer
A pudding eater
A parkin gobbler
A terrier walker
A tea drinker
A ferret keeper
A pipe smoker
A silent talker
A white rose lover

I'm right proud to be a Yorkshire man.

Jessica Lucy Lisles (8)
Birdwell Primary School, Birdwell

Yorkshire Man

A kennings poem

A parkin maker
A white rose lover
A tweed wearer
A pipe smoker
A tea drinker
A kestrel flyer
A flat cap wearer
A whippet walker
A terrier taker
A pudding eater
A silent talker
A ferret walker

I'm a proud Yorkshire man.

Caitlin Dickinson (9)

Birdwell Primary School, Birdwell

Yorkshire Man Beginning

A kennings poem

A white rose lover
A pudding eater
A terrier taker
A tea downer
A whippet walker
A flat cap wearer
A tweed wearer
A kestrel flyer
A pipe smoker
A parkin baker
A ferret walker
A silent speaker

I am a proud Yorkshire man.

Hollie Thorpe (7)
Birdwell Primary School, Birdwell

Yorkshire Man

A kennings poem

A parkin maker
A white rose lover
A tweed wearer
A pipe smoker
A tea drinker
A kestrel flyer
A flat cap wearer
A whippet walker
A terrier taker
A pudding eater
A silent talker
A ferret walker

I am a proud Yorkshire man!

Chloe Wild (7)
Birdwell Primary School, Birdwell

Yorkshire Man

A kennings poem

A whippet walker
A parkin lover
A tea lover
A flat cap lover
A pipe smoker
A terrier walker
A ferret walker
A white rose lover
A tweed wearer
A terrier taker

I'm a right proud Yorkshire man.

Lilly Holmes (7)
Birdwell Primary School, Birdwell

Yorkshire Man

A kennings poem

A pipe smoker
A flat cap wearer
A pudding eater
A terrier taker
A tea drinker
A silent talker
A tweed wearer
A parkin maker
An old shoe wearer
A kestrel flyer

I am a proud Yorkshire man.

Lucas John (7)
Birdwell Primary School, Birdwell

Yorkshire Man

A kennings poem

A whippet walker
A rose lover
A flat cap wearer
A kestrel flyer
A tweed jacket taker
A parkin eater
A ferret founder
A pipe smoker
A silent talker

I'm right proud to be a Yorkshire man.

Zak Goodhall (8)
Birdwell Primary School, Birdwell

Yorkshire

A kennings poem

A whippet keeper
A parkin winner
A tweed jacket wearer
A flat cap wearer
A rose lover
A pipe maker
A pudding eater
A tea drinker
A kestrel flyer
A ferret walker
A silent walker.

Francis Simmons (8)
Birdwell Primary School, Birdwell

Yorkshire Man

A kennings poem

A flat cap wearer
A parkin lover
A whippet walker
A kestrel flyer
A terrier walker
A pudding eater
A tea adorer
A pipe smoker
A white rose lover

I am a proud Yorkshire man.

Jenny Bebb (9)
Birdwell Primary School, Birdwell

Yorkshire

A kennings poem

A flat cap lover
A parkin lover
A whippet lover
A terrier keeper
A kestrel flyer
A pudding eater
A flat cap wearer
A Yorkshire rose taker

Am I a Yorkshire man?

Demi Crookes (7)
Birdwell Primary School, Birdwell

Yorkshire Man

A kennings poem

Flat cap wearer
A whippet walker
Flying a kestrel lover
Yorkshire tea drinker
Yorkshire pudding eater
Yorkshire terrier walker
A God's own country pipe smoker.

Isabella Wright (9) & Lucie

Birdwell Primary School, Birdwell

This Is Our World...

The scorching sun, it burns so bright,
Spreading around its golden light,
Rippling rivers and blossoming trees,
Beautiful butterflies, buzzing bees,
This is our world...

The desert, however, has little life,
The cacti's prick as sharp as a knife,
Whirling winds, storms of sand,
Covering this hard, brittle land,
This is our world...

The ocean is so very long, a sapphire blue,
Flowing with secrets, pure and true,
Animals swim happy, not sad,
Nothing about this seems to be bad,
This is our world...

The rainforest, deep, dense and compact,
Most creatures survive here, that is a fact,
The plants, they grow every which way,
Keeping the animals fed today,
This is our world...

There are many layers, the crust and the core,
That keep this world peaceful and pure,
It was made for me and made for you,
And everyone else who lives here too,
This is our world...

Reggie Butcher (11)

Buckingham Park CE Primary School, Buckingham Park

The Back Row

The back row is fun,
They really won,
When they sit in class.

They can be rude,
They can scoff food,
It's just like a free pass.

They always act cool,
Looking at the fools,
Chilling with so much ease.

They don't do their work,
At the back row, they smirk,
After all... no teachers to please!

Now for the front row,
The expectations hang low,
The fun-o-metre's not high.

The teacher's deathly glare,
She's like a grizzly bear,
She makes them act all shy.

It's like burning in hell,
Or being locked in a cell,
They're being lit on fire.

They're forced with their work,
At the front row, they lurk,
They're walking a deadly tripwire.

Carmen Douras (10)
Buckingham Park CE Primary School, Buckingham Park

Slimicorntopia

I live on a planet of unicorns,
Unicorns that don't wear any type of uniforms,
Some colours are blue,
You can't catch the flu,
Some colours are pink,
And just with a wink,
I can change the weather,
As light as a feather.

Everyone is free,
Of course, there is tea,
There is also slime,
And we can change the time,
Slime of every kind,
Slime that you can find,
Normally, the weather is warm,
Sometimes there are swarms of unicorns.

Peace and no chargers,
Money and no farmers,

There are three suns in each corner,
But only the heat you order,
It is full of unicorns and slime,
You can come any time.

Adebola Olowosale (10)

Buckingham Park CE Primary School, Buckingham Park

The Unknown Area 51

Here goes my terrific, scary and anonymous trip to Area 51
On my way to Area 51, I could see soldiers and a lot of sandy boulders
When I arrived, I could see a lot of rockets and soldiers with big pockets.

When I went inside, it was amazing, it looked like the super future
I saw UFO tests on anonymous aliens that were weird
Because of their heads, they looked like weird pets
It was night, so I asked them if they discovered the stars and Mars
I was surprised because they said yes.

I saw robo rats hiding under tanks, I wondered if they had some kind of plan
Or maybe tests on rats, UFOs or maybe aliens?
The journey was amazing and a great, great mystery.

Alan Trzcinsti (10)
Buckingham Park CE Primary School, Buckingham Park

The Most Important Person

I am an astronaut, I circle the stars
I walk on the moon, I travel to Mars
I am brave and bruised, there's nothing I fear
I am the most important person here.

I am the teacher, I teach you all day
Teach you about Santa and his big, old sleigh
I help you when you've got a tear
I am the most important person here.

I am your mum, I dress you every day
I make sure you're always on your way
I make sure you don't drink any beer
I am the most important person here.

I am me, I like drinking tea
I don't like being stung by a bee
I always like my family near
I am the most important person here.

Alicia Dashwood (11)
Buckingham Park CE Primary School, Buckingham Park

Galaxy Cats

Meow! Meow!
The galaxy cats on the stars
Flew fast and touched Mars
The sky was really dark
But they still reached the galaxy park
The galaxy cats were so fluffy
That when the rain came, they went puffy
When the sun shone down, it was so light
That the ice cream melted in delight
The ice cream was so cold
That the galaxy cats went gold
As the stars started to glisten
The galaxy cats found one odd mitten
The dark galaxy was so unknown
All the galaxy cats started to moan
After a really, really long day
They went home and ordered Subway.

Poppy Fairclough (11)
Buckingham Park CE Primary School, Buckingham Park

I Live On Mars

I live on the planet Mars,
Where people sit gazing at the stars,
I can see the moon, not too far away,
I like to visit it at least once a day,
We all know that there are footsteps on the moon,
They're mine, I swear, not that other dude's!

There are aliens and aliens all over this place
And quite frequently they ask, "Want to race?"
The Mars population isn't very high
Until one day a rocket fell out of the sky,

A strange creature hopped out the rocket and
kicked the door,
He didn't look like anything I'd seen before.

Grace Boswell (11)
Buckingham Park CE Primary School, Buckingham Park

The Moon's Question To Us From Mars

As the moon rises up high at night
So will the stars that shine bright
Let the shadows come to play
After aliens awake from sleeping all day.

As the crickets sing
As the trees dance
The fireflies prance
As the wind howls towards the glowing stars
I think the moon has a question from Mars!

In the pitch-black, stormy night sky,
Why do people not trust the dark night?
Is it because the shadows lie?
Is it because the aliens will keep you up at night?
Is it because monsters will take your soul and feed
it to the large beam of light?

Peyumi Senanayake (11)
Buckingham Park CE Primary School, Buckingham Park

Dreams

What do you do when you feel bored?
Do you pretend to kill a beast with a mystical
sword?
Or are you scaring a lion that roared?
Or shooting a dino that gracefully soared?

In your big dreams, what actually happens?
Are you the top of the team, the captain?
In your big dreams, what actually happens?
Are you a teen that's sick at rapping?

If you had godly powers, what would you do?
Would you give Trump the cold or the flu?
Or would you get Balenciaga's shoe?
And then make a bully flush his head in the loo?

Abdullah Salihu Ali (10)
Buckingham Park CE Primary School, Buckingham Park

Dear 2055

We're killing Earth and that's not fun
No one believes us kids, because we are young
Forests and jungles turning to ash within a second,
Ask Australia, they'll tell you about it.

They'll tell you how they lost all their trees
The government can't do anything so all they do is
flee
Global warming is an expensive little boat
For the last time... this is not a joke!

Dear 2055, I don't think we're gonna survive,
If you end up hearing this story, I just want to say...
We're sorry.

Kiano Stevenson (10)
Buckingham Park CE Primary School, Buckingham Park

The Danger Of The Back Row!

My class, my class, they always seem to have a blast,
But come to the back row and you'll want to move fast,
It can be dangerous, it can be fun
But all of Mrs Lowe's work becomes undone.

We can smuggle food
We can be really rude but
If you come over, we'll change your mood.

You may think the noise
Is coming from the boys
But turn around and you may think we're real toys.

We can sing in tune,
We can take you to the moon!
Whoop! Whoop!
This is the back row's groove.

Abigail Adewumi (10)
Buckingham Park CE Primary School, Buckingham Park

School On Mars

Welcome to our school on Mars,
Where all the kids are shining stars,
Children don't walk, they fly,
Pupils don't moan, they try.

This school doesn't need any rules,
Because there are no fools,
You could even bring a toy rocket,
To put in your little pocket.

All of us are lucky,
And none of us get mucky,
We don't do history,
Because it's a mystery,

You can keep your amazing cars
Because we love our school on Mars.

Tamzin Louise Aiken (11)
Buckingham Park CE Primary School, Buckingham Park

Foodtopia

Welcome to Foodtopia,
The world is so yummy.
Forget the other planets,
Don't be a dummy!

Ice cream and burgers,
All you can eat.
Chocolate and muffins,
Have a little treat.

There will be loads of jelly,
And lots of delicious cake.
It'll be enough to fill your belly,
There's also a chocolate lake!

That's it for now,
But if you want to see more,
Come to Foodtopia,
There are sweet treats galore!

Kaira Premnazeer (10)
Buckingham Park CE Primary School, Buckingham Park

Sugar Rush

We had just had dinner, now it's time for my treats
We went to the shop to get some lovely sweets
I didn't know what one to choose,
Got a race tomorrow, don't wanna lose.

I had my chocolate stars,
Or I had my Milky Bars
I had my toffee
It smelt like coffee.

I'm not going to lie, eating all that candy
Made me feel a little queasy
I hope my mum doesn't find out
If she does, she will surely shout
Wish me luck!

Tia Jade Way (11)
Buckingham Park CE Primary School, Buckingham Park

Alien Raid

I saw an alien from Mars
I think it left his hometown with the stars
His blotchy skin was a bogey-green
And his body is petite, skinny and lean.

He came in his UFO
Which emitted a gloomy glow
The small, circular lights
Gave the humans below a fright
They wondered as to what had appeared
The children and adults trembling with fear.

All of their hearts racing faster than light
Would there be an outbreak, would there be a
fight?

Michelle Bamfo (11)
Buckingham Park CE Primary School, Buckingham Park

Spring

The rain fell from the glistening tree,
It was so quiet you couldn't hear a bumblebee,
It was a particularly cold day,
In the frozen acres of May.

Animals reproducing at this time,
And eating healthy green vines,
Next, Easter came,
To celebrate Jesus' fame.

Next season, there will be lots of sun,
People running to the beach to have some fun,
T-shirts on show,
People wearing flip-flops showing their toes.

Jacob Sabine (11)
Buckingham Park CE Primary School, Buckingham Park

The KFC Fairytale

KFC is the place to be,
Go there and you will see,
You'll taste the world's best gravy,
And it will make you feel all wavy.

The chicken is very delicious,
It makes me avaricious,
As soon as the chips touch my lips,
I savour the flavour and the dip.

The range of drinks makes my mind think,
Which drink should I pick, could it be pink?
The customer service never fails
To end my amazing fairy tale.

Courtney-Skye Hogan (11)
Buckingham Park CE Primary School, Buckingham Park

Dreams

Hello, my name is Amory
I'm here to talk about my dreams, my desires
I do not want to be forgotten by the unforgiving
sands of time
To be washed away like a pebble in the river
For I want to leave my mark in this world
Make my own discovery,
Write an amazing book,
Create something to grow as a person,
We all want this and isn't that the beauty of
humanity?

Amory Ncube (10)
Buckingham Park CE Primary School, Buckingham Park

Rage Monster

I get a little competitive when playing Fortnite,
I hope my cat, Lily, is out of sight,
When I am playing 'cause it makes me mad,
And my behaviour makes her really sad,
I punched my controller into a box,
And screamed into a pair of socks,
It just makes me so furiously cross,
Even when my player does the floss,
And when I get killed by a boss.

Oscar Kennelly (11)
Buckingham Park CE Primary School, Buckingham Park

We Are In Danger

We are in danger
Yes, even you, stranger
You get in a car
Drive really far
As you turn a corner
The world gets warmer
Global warming is here
Attacking our beloved sphere
Cars are the main problem
So we need to stop them
A normal bike is better
So put back on that sweater!

Wiktoria Duszyk (11)
Buckingham Park CE Primary School, Buckingham Park

Up Above

Up above,
Past the clouds,
Without making any sounds,
Up above,
Through the sky,
Birds waiting for it to fly by,
Up above,
Into space,
Looking at the Earth's face,
Up above,
Towards the moon,
A rocket ship will land very soon.

Thanthai Child (11)
Buckingham Park CE Primary School, Buckingham Park

Save The Earth

We are killing the Earth
And people are having fun
No one believes us because we are young
Fires are spreading
Pollution is killing
People are dying
A virus is spreading
No one knows why.

Andremary Rafaela Marin (11)
Buckingham Park CE Primary School, Buckingham Park

Space

I am going to Pluto
I am seeing a UFO
I am in space
I ask the alien, "Do you want to race?"
The alien says yes
Everything goes pitch-black
I think I want a Big Mac.

Tawana Chikozho (10)

Buckingham Park CE Primary School, Buckingham Park

Dream

D rift off to sleep
R ide to Adventure Land
E ventually, you wake up
A lso gives you happy thoughts
M akes you think
S leep people, sleep.

Bradley Olatunde (10)
Buckingham Park CE Primary School, Buckingham Park

The Alien's Talent Show

Gurgle, gurgle, gurgle, pop
An alien did the vossibop
Its tentacles were green and blobby
And awful dancing was its hobby

Another monster took a stab
With arms too short to do the dab
Although it tried and tried and tried
It could not do it so it cried

The third one thought it was the boss
With lots of eyes, it did the floss
It bent over and did a guff
The judges were like, "That's enough."

The judges stood up angrily
The monsters thought they looked silly
The monsters ate the judges up
And lifted high the victory cup.

Jim West (8)
Halstow Primary School, Greenwich

Maths Is The Best

There are still many curiosities of maths today,
As there is so much to learn,
There's no time to play!
Some maths problems are hard, some are easy,
And some can make your mind go crazy!
Oh! Subtraction, addition, they muddle
mathematicians!
To solve a hard problem like that,
You have to give your brain a pat!
There are many ways of solving it,
Please do try, it keeps your brain fit.
Do you have a strategy right up your sleeve,
To solve any question you receive?
If you don't, I'll tell you mine,
Concentrate and you'll be fine.
Does it work, it does but why?
Never mind that, have a little try.
Me, myself is a lover of maths,
You might be one too perhaps.

So there *are* still curiosities about maths today,
And there *is* so much to learn,
But there is *some* time to play!

Luyang Gao (8)
Halstow Primary School, Greenwich

The Curiosity Shop

The Curiosity Shop
What a curious name
But how come it's so lonely?
So lonely and plain
It's normally filled with people and things
But now just rings without hands and hands
without rings
All those poor owners working all day and night
Have lost all their confidence, resilience and might
All those people had quit their jobs
And now all they do is eat corn on the cob
The next day, a guard came to see them and
Said it was all a mistake
And now they're working with the curiosities
By the palm tree and the lake.

Eva Shen-Barker (8)
Halstow Primary School, Greenwich

The Three Dogs

Whizzing through space
There's a real catastrophe
No human can do anything at all
It's down to the dogs
Our animal friends must save the galaxy
It's down to Chewie the Cockapoo
Cooper the Labrador
And Sylvie the Newfoundland
It's down to them
They must use their incredible noses and ears
To track down those monstrous beasts
Aliens!
Oh no! But luckily
Cooper the Labrador
Sylvie the Newfoundland and
Chewie the Cockapoo
Have saved the world.

Fleur Boughen (8)
Halstow Primary School, Greenwich

Save The Panda

Save the panda, white and black
Once they're gone they can't come back
They are wonderful and snuggly
They are as soft as a blanket
Bamboo is what they eat
So don't feed them meat
We burn down their forest
Take away their bamboo
They hardly have any babies
One or maybe two
We need to look after them
We need to protect them from danger
So save the pandas, white and black
Once they are gone, they can't come back.

Eva Murphy (8)
Halstow Primary School, Greenwich

Pets At The Vets

Here are the animals down at the vets
There are all sorts of lonely and miserable pets
Here comes a parrot with knobbly knees
Here comes a dog with a bad case of fleas
Here comes a lady bringing her pug
His face is so green - it's a grim tummy bug
Here comes a hamster that has too much fur
Here comes a kitten that can't give a purr
Here comes an earwig that pinches them all
A vet's not a peaceful place after all!

Molly Norris (7)

Halstow Primary School, Greenwich

WWII

The helpless people were ants
The helpless poor people were scary noises
The bombs were meteors
The endless cold water was a whirlwind
The fire was a dragon
The smoke was a whirlwind
The bombs were a bit of lava
The bombs were lava
The bombs were fire
The bombs were as black as night.

Amelie Yates (8)
Halstow Primary School, Greenwich

I Love Pie

Pie,
Pie,
I love pie
You love pie
I love pie
Pie,
Pie,
Apple, rhubarb
Even pear
Any flavour, we don't care!
Pie,
Pie,
I love pie
You don't like it... do not lie
Pie,
Pie,
You love pie so I love pie.

Eira Perilioglu (8)
Halstow Primary School, Greenwich

Naughty

My name is Tommy
And I'm rude to my mummy

I destroyed my house
And turned into a mouse

Other kids think I'm a pest
But I think I'm the best.

Liam Hermreck (7)
Halstow Primary School, Greenwich

Me And My Best Friend And Puppies

P uppies are cuddly and snuggly
U sing pugs to catch bugs is wrong
P uppies are snuggly and Halle says so
P uppies are so cuddly and Scarlett knows
Y es, Halle is nice and you can never ask her twice

W e all see Scarlett is lovely and very bubbly
E ven lovely people are bubbly too

L ovely puppies are cuddly puppies
O ther puppies are snuggly to friends
V ans are a favourite for puppies and they're cuddly
E very puppy is so cuddly

Y es, sure, all puppies think they are very nice
E asy for puppies to be snuggly
S nuggly and cuddly, friends with puppies.

Joyce-Joan Staines (8)

Hartlebury CE Primary School, Hartlebury

Dreams And Nightmares

D ream of Candy Land
R ace across the world
E legant monsters
A nimals escaping
M um shouting at you
S melly and rotten food

A nd have a holiday
N ever stop running
D ad is a vampire

N ightmares are the worst
I nk spilt on my new top
G oblins chasing you
H am and cheese
T oast on Mondays
M onsters lurking under the bed
A ngry wolves coming to catch you
R un away from the hairy monster
E ating too many sweets
S melly underground tunnels

Demetri Withers (8)
Hartlebury CE Primary School, Hartlebury

Football

F antastic footballs flying everywhere

O verhead kick in the goal, that's when you celebrate and slide on the floor

O n a free kick, you stand in a wall, not a brick wall, you can still fall

T raining is important, but not in your underwear

B alls everywhere, balls there, hopefully not in your goal

A fter the match, you have a snack and then go home

L eft mid going for a shot and scores a screamer

L eft defence clearing the ball away so no balls go past the keeper.

Emma Riches (9)
Hartlebury CE Primary School, Hartlebury

Animals

A t the rainforest, some animals are fierce and some are beautiful

N ames of animals can be weird but some can be magical

I t can sound a bit strange but animals are fantastical

M ammals are beautiful and dangerous and some are amazing

A t the jungle, some are cheeky and some are lazy

L ame animals are quite fascinating and some are crazy

S ome animals are predators and some and prey.

Eleanor Webber (8)

Hartlebury CE Primary School, Hartlebury

The Sea

The sea dozes calmly in the bright, burning sun,
Little waves tickle the sandy shores.
Turquoise ripples darken to cobalt
Then intense sapphire.

Storm clouds start to gather,
Covering the incandescent sun.
Vast waves crash angrily onto the sandy shore,
Overturning boats and pulling them down
Deep, deep down into the murky waters below.

Freja Palmer (9)
Hartlebury CE Primary School, Hartlebury

I Really Don't Like Spiders

I really don't like spiders
Especially the big ones
They have eight arms
That's way too many
Who needs that many?
I don't mind the dinky ones
But on second thoughts
They scurry into your curry
They scatter into your batter
They crawl onto your meatball
They bowl into your soul
I really don't like spiders!

Martha Plant (8)
Hartlebury CE Primary School, Hartlebury

Animals

A nimals are mostly wild

N ow you should look after animals very carefully

I love animals because they are cute

M y hamster's name is Cookie Monster

A n animal is either wild or a pet

L ots of animals in the wild survive

S ome animals are so tiny, like hamsters.

Olivia Steele (8)
Hartlebury CE Primary School, Hartlebury

Big Foot

In the forest, it wanders about, big and hairy
Strong and scary, then through the night
It watches over its home, hunting bats or rats
And crashing and smashing the trees
In the gentle midnight breeze
And killing in the chilling wind
Using infrasound to shock its prey
At the time of day.

Alexander Summers (9)
Hartlebury CE Primary School, Hartlebury

Laughter

L aughter is laughter

A nd no one can stop you

U nless you stop yourself

G reater times

H appiness of laughter makes joy appear

T he sound of laughter makes friends appear

E ven in the night

R eal laughter happens.

Oliver Haydon (9)

Hartlebury CE Primary School, Hartlebury

Snake

Slitheryserpents roam the land
Fat and thin all around
Some eat rats
Some eat cats
Some are the same and some are insane!
I like them a lot
One and all with spots
And dotty
That is the end of my snakey lot.

Syd Cole (9)
Hartlebury CE Primary School, Hartlebury

The Love Of My Family

F amily is nice to you

A nd maybe not your brother but you

M other will always be

I n love with pets

L oving to the moon and back

Y ummy food to fill you up to the top.

Scarlett Terry (8)

Hartlebury CE Primary School, Hartlebury

Hartlebury's The Best

Hartlebury, Hartlebury is the best
Better than the rest
Because they don't have
Hairy chests!

Ella Mulcahy (9)
Hartlebury CE Primary School, Hartlebury

Out In Space

Dramatically, the blood-red rocket leapt high into a black blanket of infinite darkness

Every single day, the sun smiles down on all the planet

When the marvellous moon orbits the sleeping Earth, spinning lazily, watching all the children wriggling in their beds

In the silent, gaping galaxy, comets majestically shoot through space

In the big, red storm of Jupiter, dust is flying here and there whilst rocks are being hurled around the prominent planet dreads

But remember, the universe is a dangerous but magical, pitch-black cabinet of endless space...

Yixiang Hou (9)
Knightwood Primary School, Chandlers Ford

Lost In Space

The sparkling stars are beautiful diamonds lost in
an infinite blanket of darkness
The raging rocket rose higher as it climbed further
and further into the moonlit sky
Curiously, the adventurous astronaut wandered
into the deadly silence of space only to find
emptiness
Gazing down at Earth, the majestic moon sat alone
waiting for someone to come
The sizzling sun roared louder than a firework
leaping into the dazzling majestic night sky
Excitedly, the elegant, beautiful shooting star
spiralled around the spectacular solar system.

Sai Mistry (10)
Knightwood Primary School, Chandlers Ford

Solar System

Moon shines brightly in the darkness of the night
Stars shooting glitter everywhere
Sun heats up the land
Mars growing red in its own gravity
Jupiter is a giant planet in the whole system
The galaxy between Mars and Venus
Saturn has sparkly spirals around him
Dotted with crystals of ice
Pluto is no longer a planet anymore
It used to be a planet but it's a very small planet
And it is poor as well as that's why Pluto isn't a planet.

Devraj Landa (9)
Knightwood Primary School, Chandlers Ford

In Space Lie The Planets

Gorgeous galaxy is dazzling light in the empty darkness

The shimmering stars shoot across the sky like diamonds

The racing rocket leapt across the dark sky

Shining sun glimmered in a blanket of darkness

The mesmerising moon spun around the peaceful Earth gently

Soaring solar system sat in the silent sky

Mesmerising Mars stood in the empty darkness

Soaring Saturn's icy rings slept in the beautiful sky.

Eloise Davies (9)
Knightwood Primary School, Chandlers Ford

Dancing Through The Solar System

A graceful galaxy swept silently through soundless space

Like goddesses, the shining stars shone down on the snoozing solar system

The thoughtless comets disappeared past Saturn, lost forever

Eclipses are golden, gleaming treasures hidden in the darkness of space

Roaring rockets speed hopefully through the flowing galaxy

The placid planets performed all night, twirling through relaxing space like gems.

Abigail Flood (10)
Knightwood Primary School, Chandlers Ford

Space

The raging rocket rammed into spinning Saturn
Supreme stars sang as mad Mercury moaned
Jupiter jogged around the sapphire that is the sun
The black hole sucked in anything nearby with glee
Super sun sent happiness to Earth in a small,
spectacular beam
The planets are a carousel, unique as they orbit
the sun
Mars is a vigorous volcano, exploding every evil
year
Darkness covered our planet, as night fell upon us.

Megan Lewis (9)
Knightwood Primary School, Chandlers Ford

Super Space

Mesmerising Mars ran across the steamy hot sun
Sparkly stars are shining like diamonds in the magical galaxy
The beautiful galaxy floated in the golden solar system
Rockets wildly danced through the icy and hot sun
The orange and red sun slowly went around the mesmerising Earth
The moon is an empty blank face jumping around the steamy hot sun
The glittery solar system bounced through the planets.

Millie Rickerd (9)
Knightwood Primary School, Chandlers Ford

Shining Space

Super sun is a flaming ball of lava that is the heat
of our solar system
Magnificent, marvellous moon majestically orbited
Earth
Like diamonds in the sky, the stars shone down on
our beautiful planet
As they slingshotted around the moon, Apollo and
their passengers were freezing to death because
the energy was turned off
The golden galaxy is as beautiful as a rainbow.

Matthew Talboys (10)
Knightwood Primary School, Chandlers Ford

The Space Solar System

Sparkling sun spiralled around the solar system with a twinkle
Marvellous moon moaned in the giant, glowing galaxy
The stars are shimmering lightbulbs brightly dancing in the darkness
Silent Saturn sat in the wind which the whooshing asteroid made
Musical Mars sang beautifully in the spectacular solar system
The galaxy was as dark as the bottom of the ocean.

Eva Thompson (10)

Knightwood Primary School, Chandlers Ford

The Planets

The marvellous moon is spinning like stars in the night sky
Stars shine brightly like mini-moons
Super Saturn spins around the solar system
Stormy Jupiter majestically tiptoes across the never-ending universe
The moon is a dark, stormy place of concrete floating around the Earth
Slowly, Pluto runs around the blazing sun.

Ben Humphrey (9)
Knightwood Primary School, Chandlers Ford

Dancing Through The Milky Way

Shimmering sun smiled softly twirling to light up the whole galaxy
Misty moon danced peacefully as it orbited around the excellent Earth
Golden galaxy is home to many amazing, peaceful planets
Swirling stars sang sweetly as the Earth drifted softly to sleep
Marvellous Mars is a raging hot planet sleeping happily in the night.

Charlotte Green (10)

Knightwood Primary School, Chandlers Ford

Our Solar System

Magnificent Mercury marches
Closest to the sun
Supersized stars
Stare down at planets
Immense asteroids zoom
At tremendous speeds
Magnificent moons sleep
Silently next to planets
Stupendous Saturn's rings
Are as thin as paper
Courageous comets crash
Curiously into Earth.

Benjamin Wasenczuk (9)
Knightwood Primary School, Chandlers Ford

Space Poem

Shimmering stars smiled in a pure black blanket of rocks
The spectacular sun shot down like a meteor on Earth
Grey, misty galaxy shimmered in the night sky
The majestic rocket screamed through the golden galaxy, jumping over hard, grey rocks
The majestic moon jogs around the Earth, jazzily.

Jake Bray (10)
Knightwood Primary School, Chandlers Ford

The Hidden World

Majestic moon shone like the brightest light
Sparkling stars shimmered in the night
Kind sun was as hot as a lightbulb
Huge Jupiter sits and watches over dwarf planets
Super rockets flew into the darkness of space
Saffron-blue Neptune sleeps at the edge of the galaxy.

Esme Cole (10)
Knightwood Primary School, Chandlers Ford

Superior Space

S peeding rockets sprint through space

P erfect planets orbit the superb sun

A wesome astronauts bounce on the moon like
  kangaroos

C razy comets run races towards Earth

E xcellent animals also surf space!

George Edwards (10)

Knightwood Primary School, Chandlers Ford

Out Of This World

O uter space, we're here again
U nknown territories await us
T wisting and turning, passing the sun

O verwhelmed with excitement, we surely must be there
F lickering through the sparkling stars, as the planet Pluto glares

T winkling, twirling through the red mist
H urtling speedily, approaching the moon
I lluminating lights in the air, fast as I glare
S wooping, swirling, sizzling in the sky, just letting the world go by

W ould we get there?
O ut of this world! We're nearly there, neon glow around spheres
R apidly racing, not long now, navigating past the astonishing ISS
L ightly landing, we've finally arrived
D eserted land, hello, your friends are here.

Kieran Brown (11)
Llwyncrwn Primary School, Beddau

Out Of This World

O ut of Earth's orbit, the red planet lies ahead
U nknown planet with its iridescent dusty bed
T ested by professionals to see if we have the courage!

O ff past the moon we fly with our floating luggage
F lying as fast as a shooting star

T he vibration is stronger than a speedy car!
H ere we are, the red planet Mars
I look out of the window and gaze at shining, shimmering stars
S oaring past Mars' two moons!

W orlds far away, different sizes and shapes, some like balloons
O verwhelmed with excitement
R eady to land in ten seconds, we're all happy with excitement
L eft with a rumble, now we land, off goes the lid
D id we make it? Yes, we did!

Tia-Leigh Norman (10)
Llwyncrwn Primary School, Beddau

Out Of This World

O ut in the vast infinity of space where all planets are born

U nknown stars await, illuminating the dead night sky

T errifying sounds while the unknown collides

O ptions are futile, ground control in a panic

F loating uncontrollably, trying to catch a breath

T his journey is now a mess

H ubble telescope picks up the disaster

I free-fall as my shuttle disintegrates

S o incredible, the glowing colours

W orld spinning, the colours collide

O nly black and flashing lights, can ground control save me?

R ocket racing back to the void that is space

L anding back to Mars, no more amazing sights

D id I just do something incredible?

George Stewart-Durose (10)

Llwyncrwn Primary School, Beddau

Out Of This World

O ut into the illuminated vast parts of space
U nknown planets are being discovered face to face
T rillions of solar systems, waiting to be found

O utstanding Earth looking like a large round pound
F ar away from Earth, we see Planet Mars

T he infinite space has numerous stars
H unting for the moon
I t's Americans against the Russians
S o it's time to land on the moon

"W e did it, boys!"
O ut of Earth's atmosphere
R oaring off like a shooting, scintillating star
L osing control because Earth's gravity is pulling us down
D own on the Earth, as we land everyone is applauding us.

Ethan Ollis (9)
Llwyncrwn Primary School, Beddau

Out Of This World

Three, two, one, blast off into the infinite unknown,
Our rocket's flames blasted like a dragon
breathing fire,
We were shooting and soaring through the sky,
Illuminated asteroids went flying by.

The stars were like tiny ants in the ebony vastness,
My apprehensive heart pounded like a drum,
The giant sun gleamed like a gargantuan
headlight.

Got to Mars and took one step,
This planet was definitely out of breath,
I fell off Mars and landed on a UFO,
The ceiling opened and there I stood, in a UFO full
of pud.

My rocket came and picked me up,
I went to Jupiter and got a little stupider,
We went to Venus, Earth and Mars and lost all our
chocolate bars,
That was the end so we went back home, telling
our poem in a thrilling tone.

Issabel Lawry (10)
Llwyncrwn Primary School, Beddau

Out Of This World

O ut past the atmosphere

U mpteen stars gleaming brightly

T housands of satellites journeying through space

O ff to the moon the astronauts go

F loating meteors skimming around the shuttle

T errifying thoughts going through their heads

H eavy suits they wear to keep them alive

I mpressive stunts the pilot masters

S atisfying colours all around

W onderful sights you can see, like Earth, Jupiter and Mars

O ff back home they all go, three, two, one, blast off!

R apidly they go back to Earth

L anding soon, happy as ever to see their families

D escending to Earth, safe and sound.

Jayden Baker (10)

Llwyncrwn Primary School, Beddau

Out Of This World

Space
Is a very vast and ebony place,
The stars are shining like no other,
The sun is like a nice warm cover,
Watching all the planets go around,
So far there is no life to be found.

The amazing sun is a ball of fire,
For that you cannot call me a liar,
But space is beautiful, that's a fact,
Even though it is jam-packed!

What is out there? We want to know,
When will aliens perform a show?
Are there any more planets out there?
How would we know?

Flying in the rocket is kind of fun,
But the danger level is one hundred and one,
Yay! We finally arrived on the moon,
I'm standing here, looking at our planet at noon.

Lailamai Evans (10)
Llwyncrwn Primary School, Beddau

The Mars Mission One

Here we go, into the unknown,
Mars will be my brand new home,
Soaring through the ebony sky,
Will we make it there alive?

We shatter through the atmosphere,
Will we get out? That I fear,
Now we're weightless, we glide in the air,
We made it through, we're nearly there!

Mars awaits as we fly through the night,
Earth waves goodbye as we lose it from sight,
We are in reach of the crimson ball,
Earth in the distance, vulnerable and small.

Overwhelmed with excitement, my heart beats
fast,
This life on Mars, how long will it last?
New ways of breathing and existing forever,
Returning to Earth will now happen never!

Robert Norfolk (10)
Llwyncrwn Primary School, Beddau

Out Of This World

Whizzing, whirling, whooping, *crash!*
The alien emerges,
As confused as a kitten,
As beady-eyed as a cat,
Where has he landed?

Illuminated dots on poles
Light his way on this alien planet,
Frozen to the spot in fright!
Face sweating,
Heart pounding!

Ahh, a human boy,
Who are you?
Tim the humanoid has come to help.
He shows the alien food and drinks,
Fizzy pop, yum,
This food is out of this world!

Next, he finds clothes and shoes,
Colourful, trendy, wow!

This coat is out of this world,
So back he flies in his bright red coat,
Slurping on a slushie,
That trip was out of this world!

Amy Algren-Carter (10)

Llwyncrwn Primary School, Beddau

Out Of This World

Out of this infinite world,
An unimaginable friend of mine
Wants to accomplish an undreamed-of mission,
To see the Earth's sunrise shine.

The stars are shining,
Like pearls in space,
He approaches the Earth,
Fear clear on his face.

Inquisitive to find out
About life on Earth,
Where would he land?
Could it be London or Perth?

His racing rocket
Speeds through the sky,
Elf-like alien,
Flying so high.

He finally landed on a deserted beach,
He couldn't believe his eyes,

An astonishing, flaming, glittering dot,
He'd finally witnessed sunrise!

Mission accomplished.

Darcey Morgan (10)
Llwyncrwn Primary School, Beddau

Out Of This World

Mystifying UFOs seen everywhere,
Yet when we look they're never there,
Photo images posted online,
For us all to see and judge in our time.

How did they get there? Where did they go?
Where are they from? What do they know?

Mars, Saturn, Jupiter and maybe Venus,
So many planets, are they hoping to see us?
Rockets, spaceships and satellites,
Or maybe they are just flying kites.

The conclusive proof we are still waiting for,
Will an unimaginable alien ever knock on our door?

Our solitary planet, so vulnerable and small,
Surely we can't be the only life on them all.

Jayden Fisher (11)
Llwyncrwn Primary School, Beddau

Out Of This World

Soaring to the extensive, illuminated sky,
Crash! I failed when I was soaring up high,
I saw a star in the universe then I fell,
I opened my eyes. I was overwhelmed, I had
landed!
It was unimaginable, I was on a planet, stranded.

Around I looked, to the ebony night sky,
Away, far away I was from Earth and up high,
This gargantuan planet had enchanted me!
I closed my eyes and nothing I could see.

I opened my eyes, I was back at NASA,
In my rocket ship, going faster,
Today is the day I'm going to the moon,
With luck on our side, we will be there soon!

Aimee Hearse (10)
Llwyncrwn Primary School, Beddau

Out Of This World

Out I went, into the limitless vastness of space,
The stars shining like iridescent diamonds in the
sky,
As I watched our little blue planet go by,
Rockets rapidly racing into the abyss.

Planets dancing around the illuminated sun,
I stared, amazed, at mystical Mars,
An astonishing flare flickered from a gleaming
light,
What was this? Would I survive?

It was a UFO, we stood there surprised,
Out came an alien, what a shock!
I glared at the creature, it stood there still,
It entered its spaceship and zoomed away!
Will it ever be seen on another day?

Keeley Webb (10)
Llwyncrwn Primary School, Beddau

Out Of This World

O ut of this world
U nder the light
T hese illuminated planets shine oh so bright

O ver and under
F ar and wide

T here are nine planets that never collide
H opping and jumping
I n and around
S hooting stars race towards the ground

W hirling and swirling
O ut into space
R apidly racing at a speedy pace
L ighting the heavens, the meteors fly
D arkness has gone as they light the sky.

Charlie Reeves (11)
Llwyncrwn Primary School, Beddau

The Wonderful World Of Space

Three, two, one, blast off!

There I am, on the rocket,
I am having a trip of a lifetime,
Almost there, I think to myself,
It is as ebony as a deep, dark coal mine.

I can't help but gaze at the planets,
Venus, Jupiter and Mars,
Shooting through the universe, the rocket is a gannet,
Swallowing everything in sight.

The rocket races rapidly through the illuminated stars,
We are still miles away 'til we reach Mars,
Let's just hope this trip is successful,
The rocket charges through the universe, it's a raging bull.

Ben Gilley (10)
Llwyncrwn Primary School, Beddau

Out Of This World

Out of this world, entering space,
On a mission to find Planet Fusion,
The azure-blue ball glitters in the distance,
As we blast through the stars on our journey.

No other humans have landed before,
Terrifying thoughts flew through my mind,
Earth was discovering Fusion,
Got closer, there was no going back.

Meteors and satellites passed us by,
By glowing like diamonds in the dark black sky,
At last we landed, my heart beat like a drum,
Mission accomplished, the journey was done.

Ethan Freeman-Jones (11)

Llwyncrwn Primary School, Beddau

Out Of This World

I was in my rocket and there I saw
An unknown planet,
But not with one moon, but forty-four!
Neon pink and luminous blue,
Staring out the window to take a look,
Then I took my first step,
When I did, I was in shock!
It was scorching hot,
The stars danced around the planet,
They waltzed through space,
They passed comets of granite,
And did a race,
After, I had to go home,
Back I went to my ship,
I was sad, I had to go alone,
What an adventure to have in one night!

Isabelle Shearer (10)

Llwyncrwn Primary School, Beddau

Out Of This World

The sky at night
Is a sight to behold,
To see all the stars
That shine so bright.

With stars in front and stars behind,
And planets far and near,
I'd sail my yacht around the rings
Of Saturn with a cheer.

I look at the galaxy,
It seems to me
That it is a nicer chocolate
Than Cadbury's!

Georgia Thomas (10)
Llwyncrwn Primary School, Beddau

My Home

H ome is a place to be free
O pen doors for you
M um and Dad there to help
E very day wake up free again

A joyful day, always
N ight and day, always happy
D ay full of love

F ighting turns to happiness
A lways helping each other
M indful parents there for sure
I love my family so much
L ove spreads around the house
Y ou are leaving but you will have a pal.

Oliver Jones (10)

Manston Primary School, Crossgates

Treat Our World Right

Our world is our home
So don't even moan
It's a wonderful place
For all the human race

So no littering
Or our world won't be glittering
So sing with joy
And bring happiness to every girl and boy

Let the trees grow and
The wind blow
So keep the world beautiful
Lovely and colourful

Think with your mind
And be very kind
Because the world is amazing
And think of all the people
You will be saving.

Emma Maloney (10)
Manston Primary School, Crossgates

The Environment

S tinky gases from the air
A nd the litter down there
V ile graffiti in the streets
E vil people making the world deadly

T he homeless people begging for money
H urting people inside and out
E arth will come to an end

W e're destroying the Earth
O rdinary seas have now changed
R est of the world
L iving on the edge
D o it, before it's too late.

Lily Banks (9)
Manston Primary School, Crossgates

Gaming Fortnite

G ames are technology

A re good things to play

M aking objects

I maginations are open

N ow time for Fortnite

G aming every day

F ortnite all night

O rganising guns

R PGs firing at the buildings

T he people building 4x4s

N ow save the world

I conic does the job

T ry to get the Victory Royale

E nd of fighting, get back to lobby.

Dominic Carlos Azevedo (9)

Manston Primary School, Crossgates

No-Man's-Land

N obody survives here in No-Man's-Land
O h, how many of my friends have died?

M y enemies are getting closer, step by step
A m I going to die?
N o-Man's-Land is the worst
S o many have not survived

L and is becoming trenched and trenched
A nd some have just survived
N ow it's almost over
D etermined to stay alive.

Katie Froggatt (9)
Manston Primary School, Crossgates

The Earth

The Earth is like life
Earth is like eating
Earth is like a star in the sky
A planet awaits for God
The Earth is like a Christmas present to us from
God
How we keep the world clean

Earth has jungles, trees and water
The Earth has tons of animals, countries, people
and houses
Our planet was given to us
Living on Earth is hard for people here
Earth gives us trees to live and breathe.

Jack Kilcoyne (10)
Manston Primary School, Crossgates

Leeds United

L oud fans

E lland Road

E lectric support

D allas, the best free-kick taker

S hortest players but still the best

U nited we are

N ever quit, never will

I an Poveda, tricky and skilful

T yler Roberts the Welshman

E very player works to the standard

D evelop skills.

Freddie Laycock (10)
Manston Primary School, Crossgates

Leeds United

Our Captain Cooper
Costa as fast as a cheetah
Kiko keeping us in the game
Pablo scoring the screamers
Bielsa leading us to victory
Philips as strong as a rhino
Bamford making the runs
Klitch behind for the rebounders
White clearing the ball for a clean sheet
Harrison assaulting people
Dallas taking the free kicks.

Zac Brennan (10)
Manston Primary School, Crossgates

Dogs Are Cute

D ogs are cute
O h so fluffy
G as smells
S o disgusting

C lever rounding the sheep for the farmer
O rganising the animals
L ying in the grass, chilling out
L icking their water as they thirst
I ntelligent dogs do the job
E xcited dogs like to play.

Archie Charles Partner (9)
Manston Primary School, Crossgates

World Wars

W orking hard for soldiers
O f the Great War
R aging towards enemy fire
L ives that are gone
D oomed in the world

W eeping about those who died
A dmiring the brave
R emembering those who died
S urviving it is too hard, dying is too easy.

Avaneesh Gupta (9)

Manston Primary School, Crossgates

Gymnastics

G irls and boys
Y ears of training
M anager helps
N ew moves
A thletes
S tretch jump
T uck jump
I ndividual things
C artwheel
S traddle on.

Grace Hooks-Sellers (10)

Manston Primary School, Crossgates

Friends

An informal word is a mate
A friend who fights on your side is an ally
A friend who works with you is a partner
Someone you don't know is an acquaintance
The opposite is an enemy
And a best friend is like a sibling.

Summer Orme (10)

Manston Primary School, Crossgates

Tommas The Cat

Tommas the cat
Has a red hat
He played with some silk
Then sipped some milk
He glimpsed some cheese
So he felt very pleased
But it tasted like peas
So the small, spotty cat
Went off to find a rat.

Isla Wishart (9)
Manston Primary School, Crossgates

The Bugatti And Lamborghini Racing

A Bugatti and Lamborghini
Were racing on a track
But the Bugatti won because
The Lamborghini's tyres needed changing
Then the Lamborghini had to pay the Bugatti.

Michael Azevedo (9)

Manston Primary School, Crossgates

My Sister, Phoebe

P erfect Phoebe

H ilarious

O verdramatic

E xcellent at reading

B ossy as can be

E normous Harry Potter fan - my sister.

Scarlett Guilfoyle (10)

Manston Primary School, Crossgates

A Friend's Dream

I had a friend called Pie
Whose dream was to fly
Instead of him flying
He ended up crying
He bought some wings
And flew to the kings
And from that time
His new dream was to climb.

Hubert Cybulski
Paddox Primary School, Rugby

My Angel In The Sky

Nan, my friend, my heart, my soul,
The pain I have, I cannot control,
You are my angel in the sky,
I cannot stop the tears I cry,
I feel so lost without you,
Now I don't know what to do,
I feel so empty and alone,
I miss the way you used to moan,
I would give anything to have you here,
I really do miss you, dear,
I miss you more than words can say,
I think about you every day,
I'm sorry for all I did wrong,
You were a woman that was so strong,
You took everything in your stride,
For that I truly have so much pride,
To think I had a nan like you.
I miss you Nan I really do,
Now it's time to say goodbye,
You are my angel in the sky.

Tammie Carlmain (11)
Pennyhill Primary School, West Bromwich

My Fantasy Land

What a wonderful world it would be,
If it was full of my fantasies,
As every time I go into my mind,
There is always a surprise I will find.

At times, I meet an ultramarine unicorn or fairy,
But sometimes I meet something extremely scary,
So I close my eyes and count to ten,
And I'm transported to every child's haven.

With long, luscious lollipop trees,
It's a wonderful sight to see,
And don't worry if it rains,
It's only pink Lucozade.

With a river made out of hot chocolate,
You can drink it out of a golden goblet,
So I close my eyes and count to ten,
And I'm back in the normal world again.

Sachroop Atwal (9)

Pennyhill Primary School, West Bromwich

The World Of Wildlife

W   is for wildflowers that grow where no one goes

I   is for insects that help nature in wonderful ways

L   is for the lovely colours that sparkle all around

D   is for the darkness that protects the wild creatures at night

L   is for the life that fills our world, all around, from the smallest creature to the largest

I   is for the incredible animals fighting against the battles that always threaten their extinction

F   is for the fantastic teamwork and strength that our world can show

E   is for Earth, where we all live - man, animal, plants and all of nature combined.

Kelly-Ann Spoors (8)

Pennyhill Primary School, West Bromwich

The Boggler

A loud and naughty Boggler,
Who likes to scream and play,
But if you like to go to farms,
You might find him digging in hay!

A multicoloured Boggler,
Who shines just like the sun,
Rainbows follow him around,
For lots of magical fun.

If you spot the Boggler,
And can't believe your eyes,
Call your friends to come and see,
And share the big surprise!

The Boggler will take you on a journey,
You'll be whirled, twirled and swirled,
You'll see all of the faraway places
That make up our amazing world.

Molly Troth (8)
Pennyhill Primary School, West Bromwich

Our Responsibility

The Earth is extremely great,
But if we don't take care, it'll be too late,
The plants, the flowers, everything,
It's God's creation,
Yet it's our generation.

We used to die of old age,
But now we die over climate change,
There must be a solution,
To end this horrible pollution,
We have to protect our Earth,
Think of how much it's worth.

Don't throw your rubbish on the floor,
Or our world will be out of the door.

Maryam Khan (11)
Pennyhill Primary School, West Bromwich

The Day Before Christmas

In the dead of night, a reindeer flies high,
Carrying Father Christmas across the night sky,
Nobody sees them but half-munched carrot sticks
Shows that old Father Christmas has brought your festive fix.

With beautiful, amazing wrapping and ribbons galore,
Father Christmas will get what you asked for,
Oh, how we fantastically love Christmas, it can never come round too soon,
Father Christmas came after noon.

Nancy Chidera Ozoemena Ugochukwu (9)
Pennyhill Primary School, West Bromwich

Bushfires

Australia is burning down,
It's destroying such a well-known town,
We need help with water,
Not some money from celebrities,
It's useless, there is nothing we can do,
People dying like it's a world war,
Losing homes, animals too,
Firefighters bleeding and dying,
Losing their lives, their family as well,
All they can do is fight for their country,
Fierce flaming fires are taking over.

Ellie-Mai Bernice Gibson
Pennyhill Primary School, West Bromwich

The Soldier's Sacrifice

Our world was full of pain,
Very different from what it is today,
Innocent bodies were killed every day,
Gunshots were heard from far away, leaving
children in dismay.

The strong soldiers saved our lives,
But some people don't recognise,
It's too bad we can't apologise,
We live here in this paradise,
Thanks to the soldier's sacrifice.

Anointed Reginald (10)
Pennyhill Primary School, West Bromwich

Hogwarts

H appy and a mysterious cloud
O ptimistic people
G ryffindor is the best
W easleys have ginger hair
A lbus Dumbledore is the best wizard ever
R ubeus Hagrid looks after magical creatures
T om Riddle is Voldemort
S lytherin is the worst.

Jaiden Jassi (8)
Pennyhill Primary School, West Bromwich

Don't Be Bad

Even if you are bad,
Never be sad,
Although you might be a big lad,
Always look up to your dad.

Never be bad,
You could get hurt,
And that would be sad,
Maybe you should
Look up to Chad.

Even if you like to draw,
Always look out for the poor,
You never know who has been
Kicked out of the front door.

Jayden Burns (10)
Pennyhill Primary School, West Bromwich

Galaxy

G roup of stars squished up high
A nd lots of planets up high
L ike an X-ray, illuminated by lights
A stronauts wandering up high
X -rayed lights shining luminously bright
Y onder, stars over there.

Amanpreet Kaur (10)
Pennyhill Primary School, West Bromwich

What's Above?

It has forty-eight eyes,
It tells a lot of lies,
It's really tall and skinny,
It has a pal that is named Minney.

What is that in the sky? Take cover,
Don't forget to help your mother,
What an odd ship,
It's good it didn't touch my lip.

Marcell Samuels (11)
Pennyhill Primary School, West Bromwich

Fire

You're steaming hot,
You can melt a pot,
You always glow bright red,
You're hot enough to burn my bread.

You make lots of smoke,
This makes me cough and choke,
You make me run away, all panicked and scared,
Like a headless bear.

Iisha Egan (9)
Pennyhill Primary School, West Bromwich

The Snow Leopard

Very white,
Fast run,
Spotty body,
Pointy ears,
Fast, furious,
Astounding hunters,
Cool colours,
Eats meat,
Kills people,
Very cool.

Kirat Singh (9)
Pennyhill Primary School, West Bromwich

Seasons

At winter time, I see them falling from the sky,
When they touch the ground, they make no sound!
All the snowflakes make me very chilly,
I catch one on my tongue,
It makes me feel like I'm in a winter wonderland.

At summer time I see the great, golden sun
Beaming blinding light through my window,
It shines as bright as a diamond,
All the flowers have grown,
As pretty as butterflies.

At spring time, I see all the animals coming out of
hibernation,
Such as bunnies, hedgehogs,
Squirrels and owls, so cute!
It could be sunny or rainy,
But I would prefer it to be quite sunny.

At autumn time, I see the leaves falling off all the
life-saving trees,
All the leaves are just laying on the floor in distress,
But thanks to spring, all the flowers then grow
back.

Inayah Jeffers (9)

Pheasey Park Farm Primary School, Great Barr

Nightmares And Dreams

N o noise to be heard
I magination runs wild
G ather my thoughts and
H ope to sleep
T hinking of tomorrow
M aking sure I know my dance
A rranging steps in my head
R epeating the rhythm in my bed
E xhausted from the worries I have
S leep and dream of how good I am.

A spire to be better and
N ever give up
D etermined to be the best I can.

D reaming of dancing and
R eaching for the stars
E xcited and confident to
A chieve my goals
M aking my dreams come true and
S hine like a star.

Leila-Rose Ferguson (9)
Pheasey Park Farm Primary School, Great Barr

My Amazing Christmas Time

Come with me to celebrate the best time of the year,
If I am naughty, I may end up with a tear,
We could decorate the Christmas tree,
Whilst drinking hot chocolate, just you and me,
Imagine if we saw Santa's shiny sleigh,
Whilst making reindeer out of clay,
Come to my house for Christmas dinner,
Then play some games to see who's the winner,
I love seeing my family at Christmas time,
I got a present from Santa, he's started giving slime,
We ate Christmas dinner, it was delish',
Don't walk under mistletoe unless you want a kiss,
We can sit around and sing and cheer,
Whilst the adults sit around drinking all the beer.

Heidi Hunter (9)
Pheasey Park Farm Primary School, Great Barr

All About Elephants

E lephants are found in India and Africa

L egs are strong and thick to hold up the large body

E ars that are huge, which flap in the wind

P oachers hunt elephants for ivory in their tusks

H ead as hard as a wood block and the wisest of them all

A t the end of the trunk are two little spouts

N ostrils are the name of the spouts that spurt water into their mouth

T runks are long enough to touch the floor and swing from side to side.

Kyle Ball (9)

Pheasey Park Farm Primary School, Great Barr

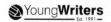

One Crisp Morning

It was a crisp morning,
The sky was blue,
Blackbirds chirped,
And robins sang just for you.

I went to town,
The church bells were ringing,
Up in the graveyard
Choirs were singing.

As I walked on the street,
There wasn't a sound,
All you could hear,
People kicking the ground.

It started to rain,
Then there was a storm,
I made my way back home,
Where it's cosy and warm.

The storm passed by,
But there was thunder,
It was even worse,

Worse than a blunder.
My life was perfect,
Perfect as can be,
Until the day you left
Me.

Ella Greenhill (9)
Pheasey Park Farm Primary School, Great Barr

Football Striker

F lick it up
O ver his head
O ver my head
T ouch down to the feet
B all control
A mazing pace down the wing
L ovely skills like Lionel Messi
L eft foot pass

S traight to the striker
T ricks two defenders
R ight foot pass
I nto the box
K iran passes it
"E rr," the defender tries to put him off
R ight into the top corner.

Liam Hegney (9)
Pheasey Park Farm Primary School, Great Barr

The Seasons Of The Year

First comes winter,
It makes lots of joy,
Then you get a splinter,
Santa will bring you a toy,
At this time of year.

Spring comes after,
It's a beautiful sight to see,
Then comes laughter,
From a little, tiny bee,
At this time of year.

The next season is full of sun,
And its name is summer,
You can make a bun,
Or even be a drummer,
At this time of year.

Last is autumn,
The sky is full of clouds,
Leaves fall on the bottom,
Of the giant crowds,
At this time of year.

Olly Bryant (9)
Pheasey Park Farm Primary School, Great Barr

Dislikes And Likes

I like playing football,
And I like playing basketball,
Also I like playing dodgeball,
You can see that they all end in ball.

If someone is bad at playing,
You shouldn't take the mick out of them,
No one will force you to play it,
People think that they're lit
At playing football.

People might have trouble,
But I don't, I'm good,
When I have a shot,
The ball goes, *bang!*
You can play what you want to play.

Eli Richards (10)
Pheasey Park Farm Primary School, Great Barr

Best Friends

B elieve in each other forever
E verlasting memories
S tick together
T ill the day we die.

F riendship never ends
R ely on one another, never cry
I n my heart there will always be a place for you
E very day I think about you
N ever want to lose you
D ays without you are hard
S tay together for life.

Isabelle Forrester (10)
Pheasey Park Farm Primary School, Great Barr

Footballers

Footballers are great,
Some just use the ball as bait,
And it gets the defenders in a state,
Messi just wants to dominate.

Football is the best!

Footballers are awesome,
And some are very troublesome,
However, some just want to look handsome,
The defenders are fearsome.

Football is the best!

Footballers are talented,
Some are very committed,
And some leave defenders deserted,
Oh no! They've scored a goal!

Corban Sargent (9)
Pheasey Park Farm Primary School, Great Barr

A Swimmer's Poem

Seven times a week,
I practise my swimming technique,
I swim laps up and down the pool,
And my gold goggles look really cool.

Backstroke is my favourite style,
I like to swim it all the while,
When I swim butterfly,
My arms reach up to the sky.

I keep up my fastest pace,
I really hope I win the race,
My eyes can see the precious metal,
Of the winner's shiny gold medal.

Henry Deavall (10)
Pheasey Park Farm Primary School, Great Barr

Rainstorm

R aindrops drip-drop on my shoes
A nd more drops fall in ones and twos
I think of all my friends inside
N ot me, I think, I shall not hide
S tormy weather makes me run
T o puddles outside, it is so much fun
O n rainy days, I'll always be
R unning around for all to see
M ud splashes and covers me!

Lara Aziz (10)
Pheasey Park Farm Primary School, Great Barr

Unicorn

U nique and beautiful, you are a mysterious
creature

N atural and graceful, strong yet gentle

I ncredibly intelligent and standing proud

C ute and cuddly with a flowing white mane

O h, how your horn glistens magically in the sun

R unning elegantly across the land you go

N ever to be tamed, you're always free.

Niamh Brayson (9)

Pheasey Park Farm Primary School, Great Barr

Jack Grealish

J ump into a football kit
A pply the boots
C heck all of the things
K eep staying calm

G et ready for the match
R un to warm up
E xplain to the team
A im for the goal
L et the ball fly
I nspire the team
S cream for the ball
H ammer into the net!

Rohan Child (9)
Pheasey Park Farm Primary School, Great Barr

Koalas

K ind koalas being injured by the boiling bushfires that are as hot as a hot tub

O pen eyes watching out for the bushfires

A ustralian people pray for the dying koalas

L ively koalas turn into sad koalas

A mazing koalas unfortunately die in the bushfires

S aved koalas that have been saved by the firefighters.

Sabrina Alizadah (10)

Pheasey Park Farm Primary School, Great Barr

Dreamer

I have a dream,
Said Martin Luther King,
It wasn't a nightmare,
Or a scream.

It will change the world,
Forever,
Now look around,
Only sixty years later.

You have to believe,
And be determined,
Imagine what you achieve,
Be brave and stand tall,
That's all.

If four words made a difference,
Your words could too,
So go on, make a change,
You might do some good.

Hollie Venner (10)
Pheasey Park Farm Primary School, Great Barr

All About Summer And Winter

S unny weather

U plifting

M ore daylight

M usic festivals

E ating loads of ice lollies

R osy cheeks from the sun

W hite snow

I cy roads

N icely wrapped presents

T obogganing down the hill

E arly night on Christmas Eve

R eally cold!

Carrie Davis (9)

Pheasey Park Farm Primary School, Great Barr

Spider

S piders crawling up your skin

P eople are scared of them

I am not scared of them because they are funny

D id you know, spiderwebs may look thin but they are not?

E very day a spider makes a new web

R ight now, there are lots of spiders in your house

S ome are big and some are tiny.

Lilly Hunt (10)

Pheasey Park Farm Primary School, Great Barr

When I Grow Up

Someday soon, when I grow up,
I'll have a job to do,
I could write a book or be a cook,
Or work inside a zoo.

I may want to drive a bus,
Or teach children to read,
I may load a train,
Or even fly a plane.

I may fight a fire,
Or be a doctor too,
Or build my house.

I will work and learn
Until it's my turn
To find the right job for me.

Layla Babbington (10)

Pheasey Park Farm Primary School, Great Barr

At Christmas

C oming together with your family
H aving a happy holiday
R unning around in the snow
I n your house are presents
S inging carols all day
'T is the season to be jolly
M aking happy memories
A ngel on top of the Christmas tree
S anta's on his way.

Kodie Webb (9)
Pheasey Park Farm Primary School, Great Barr

Football

F riendly

O ver-exciting game

O pposition running at you

T easing the opposition with the ball

B ooting the ball makes me feel good

A t every game you win, draw and lose

L ots of people like football

L et your joy spread.

Liam Durrant (10)

Pheasey Park Farm Primary School, Great Barr

Spring

S pring is a beautiful season
P retty birds start to sing
R obin red breast with babies under its wing
I see daffodils and tulips that are small
N ow it's all bright, I see no more
G o to a field and see spring bloom at its best.

Ella Horsley (10)
Pheasey Park Farm Primary School, Great Barr

All About Summer

S unny days, late nights,

U mbrella left in house,

M ore daylight,

M usic festivals,

E at lots of cold ice lollies,

R osy cheeks from the sun,

Sun is as bright as a light,

No need to rush, it's the longest day of the year.

Sydney Davis (9)

Pheasey Park Farm Primary School, Great Barr

Easter Time

E aster celebrates the resurrection of Jesus
A n Easter egg is the symbol of new life
S pecial treats for you and me
T he Easter bunny goes, hop hop hop
E veryone has fun
R emember, the Lord was taken away and then brought back.

Ruby Mya Francis (9)
Pheasey Park Farm Primary School, Great Barr

Food

Food is tasty,
Food is fun,
Food fills up my tum.

Bacon is nice,
Bacon is awesome,
I tasted some and then I bought some.

Eggs are nice,
Eggs are tasty,
And when it's so tasty, it makes me hasty.

Pasta's great,
Pasta's fun,
And when I eat it, I'm finally done!

Alfie Gardner (10)
Pheasey Park Farm Primary School, Great Barr

Jumbo Jet

J et planes in the sky
U nder and over clouds
M any people go on holiday
B lasting fast
O n to other countries far

J oyful days spent watching planes
E njoyable sight to see
T ruly the best.

Ethan Wood (9)
Pheasey Park Farm Primary School, Great Barr

Friends

Friends are caring,
Friends are loving,
I hope everyone has a friend,
And if you don't, I'm just there!

Don't be shy,
Don't be scared,
We will be friends until the end!

So come on over and let's meet,
Because having a friend is just a treat.

Amelia Baingana (10)
Pheasey Park Farm Primary School, Great Barr

Football

F un for everyone

O ff the crossbar

O ver the goal keeper

T ake the shot

B end it like Beckham

A fter I scored, I celebrated

L ong shot

L uckily it wasn't a penalty!

Dexter Leathem (9)
Pheasey Park Farm Primary School, Great Barr

Animal Loves

A lligators attack antelope

N ewts need nutritional food

I guana, ice, icicle

M onkeys move around mischievously

A nteaters ate ants

L ions like live meat

S nakes slither swiftly!

Alexander Williams (9)

Pheasey Park Farm Primary School, Great Barr

When I Grow Up

When I grow up, I would like to be
A footballer who scores goals with glee,
Playing for my country,
Top scorer for my team,
It's every young kid's dream,
So, until that day I will keep on training,
Even if it's windy and raining!

Jacob Bryant (10)
Pheasey Park Farm Primary School, Great Barr

Space

S pace is a wonderful place
P laces in space are different
A ny planet could blow up at any time
C ookies have just been made in space
E very planet has a different name and a different size.

Haillie Hobson (9)

Pheasey Park Farm Primary School, Great Barr

Football

F ootball is my hobby

O ver the fields we play

O n TV, families watch

T ackling is my aim

B ouncing the ball into the goal

A im for the goal

L oud from the crowd

L ovely football is the best!

Jack Lloyd-Roberts (9)

Pheasey Park Farm Primary School, Great Barr

Dinosaur Parade

Triceratops in a top hat,
Stegosaurus patting a cat,
Tyrannosaurus wearing a crown,
Brontosaurus dressed like a clown,
Soon they'll be ready to go, when the music is
played,
They will all be marching in the dino parade.

Daisy Hollyoake (9)
Pheasey Park Farm Primary School, Great Barr

About My Family

F amily and friends were hanging out
A nd they were having fun
M y family are the best
I love my family
L ove my sisters
Y es, I love all of my family!

Lacey Pritchard (10)
Pheasey Park Farm Primary School, Great Barr

Autumn

In autumn,
The leaves are ruby-red,
In autumn, the crispy leaves are bright red
And fall off the tree,
And dance in the wind,
Brown conkers are spread all over the floor,
It's not quite winter yet.

Malachi Jagirdar (10)
Pheasey Park Farm Primary School, Great Barr

Food And Drink

Cereal without milk is like,
Toast without jam,
Bread with no butter,
Or bread with no ham.

A milkshake without cream is like,
A tea bag without water,
Sangria with no fruit,
Or coffee with no sugar.

Lilly-May Jordan (9)
Pheasey Park Farm Primary School, Great Barr

I Have A Dream

I have a dream to be an author,
To be a zoo keeper,
I have a dream to be an artist,
To be a creative girl,
I have a dream to be a dancer,
To be a singer,
I have a dream to be,
To be anything.

Lucy Allan (9)
Pheasey Park Farm Primary School, Great Barr

Danger In Space

A ruby-red rocket flying through shimmering stars
Two brave spacemen with plans to go very far

Spinning around Mars' atmosphere like a merry-go-round
Suddenly, a rocky asteroid hits them to the ground

Disaster! They crash with a smash and a tumble
They are sad and upset and they grumble

Unexpectedly, a bright blue spaceship appears
The radio works, a man says, "We've come to rescue you, don't fear!"

The rescue rocket takes them back to Earth in a flash
On no, another disaster! They land in the cold sea with a giant splosh!

Joshua James Hobson (10)
Sherburn Hungate Community Primary School, Sherburn In Elmet

Cosmic Disco

In the stillness of the night sky,
The cosmic disco begins
With Jupiter's rings spinning
Like DJ discs, round and round

The stars elegantly prance around the Milky Way
galaxy
As mortifying Mars and its moons rock and roll
around the sun

Bright, beautiful colour
Makes the planets who they are
Reds, blues, yellows
Colours galore!

As the party comes to a close,
The planets and stars settle in their spots
For another normal day.

Mary Herridge (10)
Sherburn Hungate Community Primary School, Sherburn In
Elmet

Spectacular Space

In the middle of the dead, dark night
A sassy alien dramatically whipped their fabulous pink wig
Through the dark, shimmering sky
The aliens invaded all the galaxies in the solar system
So they could become kings of the galaxies
All the stars were shooting through the sky
Like jumping ballerinas
The planets had a disco
On the galaxy Milky Way dance floor
All the planets were beautifully bobbing around.

Holly Elizabeth Hodcroft (9)

Sherburn Hungate Community Primary School, Sherburn In Elmet

Space

At midnight, aliens start zooming through the
galactic galaxy
To discover new planets
The bright, shimmering stars dancing magically on
the dancefloor of infinity
To celebrate existence
The milk-white moon shining in the pitch-black sky
like a lightbulb
The boiling hot sun as orange as a carrot
Icy rings surround Saturn
Like a giant hula hoop.

Vanessa Subaciute (9)
Sherburn Hungate Community Primary School, Sherburn In
Elmet

The Sound Collector

Based on 'The Sound Collector' by Roger McGough

At school this morning, a stranger came
Dressed all in black
We didn't know his name
He took all of our sounds and never came back
The silence was just not right
The clicking of pen lids
The sound of excited reception children
The singing of joyful kids

The clatter of cutlery
The pitter-patter of the rain
The sound of boiling curry
And Mr Jones cleaning the windowpane

The slamming of the classroom doors
The ticking of the clock
The scraping of the chairs
The turning of the lock
The flapping of the whiteboards
The slurping of the teacher's tea

The scrunching of paper
The buzzing of a bee

The whooshing of the air vent
The beep of the reception door
The munching of yummy food
And the scraping of feet on the floor

This morning, a stranger dropped by
Without giving his name
He left us in quiet nothingness
School life will never be the same.

Arjun Sond (10)
St James CE Primary School, Birmingham

Bad Girls Inspires Me Because...

Now, before I start this poem
I just want to say hi
Okay, Bonjour, hello, s'up?
Sorry, I am letting time pass by!

Bad Girls inspires me because
It makes me think to stand up
To do what is right and you might
Agree with me, yup!
It is about a girl called Mandy
Who gets bullied by three mean girls
But the worst is Kim who is very mean
And her skin is as white as pearls

Then a girl called Tanya
Becomes Mandy's mate
She gets the bullies in trouble
By telling Mrs Kate

This is the end of the poem
I hope you read it well
And if you get bullied
Remember, to always tell!

Maria Malhi (10)

St James CE Primary School, Birmingham

We Can

Boys and girls
We all have a choice,
That's why we all have a voice
And we will all have our night,
If we choose our path right
We can be on TV,
Like Oprah Winfrey
If the truth is told,
Our smarts won't grow old
Everything takes practice,
If we don't let anything distract us
If you want to be the best, I will show you how
And you will leave people with a 'wow'
I want to be a nurse and
I won't make it worse
That's why I want to help
I won't make you yelp.

Monet Wright (10)
St James CE Primary School, Birmingham

Our Sky Is Blue

Our sky is blue and yes, that's true
I made this poem just for you
And I know our friendship will last us long
Because we play all day long
Just to make sure that you know
We sometimes play in the snow
Our sky is blue and yes, that's true
I know me and you love to dance
And sometimes prance
Come with me, I'll treat you the best I can
And that's my plan
That's it for now
It's time to say bye-bye.

Alimah Begum (8)
St James CE Primary School, Birmingham

Blaze Is In The Race

Blaze the alien is about to enter a cosmic race
She's got flaming red hair, it's totally amaze
But I really hope it won't make her sweat
I know she'll win, do you want to bet?

The race is starting to go, go, go!
"Come on Blaze! Don't go slow-mo!"
Around Jupiter, through the meteor belt
Past the sun, careful you don't melt!

Oh, what's that up ahead?
It's my warm and cosy bed
Just behind the finish line, it's calling my name
I've won! The galaxies will know my fame

Even today, if you look up high
You'll see Blaze shooting through the sky
Always on a hunt, looking for a race
She's a glowing red cannonball in space!

Anamika Ullas Nair (10)
Sunnylands Primary School, Carrickfergus

Winter And Spring

Clear, cold, shimmering, frosty water
Fiery, furry, red squirrels
Arctic foxes hunting nightly pray

Huge, melting pearl moon
Blue midnight star-covered sky
Mountains covered in sugar snow

Earth's snow blanket fades away
Tiny baby birds see light
Leaves return to lonely trees

Fresh green grass slowly growing
Flowers blooming, big, bold, beautiful
Bright blue warming sky.

Eliza Smeed (9)
Tollcross Primary School, Edinburgh

Autumn

Leaves falling... Robins chirping
Foxes in brackens, bunnies in holes
Wolf moon comes and goes
Owls sleep, owls awaken
Orange leaves beam into the sunlight
Cold air flows around the city
Of trees and homes

The moon comes to life
Foxes start hunting for their nightly prey
Rats run, creatures
Awaken and some go to sleep

Autumn the season
Of fall.

Martha Crawford (9)
Tollcross Primary School, Edinburgh

Winter

The frosty river looks like ice shining
Through the land and slippery as soup
Shining through are hands
Tickling, wiggling like a soft feather

The sky is like shiny, blue water
Glowing above us!!

The animals are not out much
Some are hibernating
And lots are hunting!

The plants die and
The glorious, green plants are gone!

Abdulaziz Softa (9)
Tollcross Primary School, Edinburgh

Winter And Spring

Crystalized leaves blowing around wildly
Hares running frantically, searching for shelter
Desperately, birds search for food
A seized up, frozen lake
Winter elegance

Flowers embroidered in grass patchwork
Sun covering trees with a golden glaze
Daffodils seeping through muddy Earth
Ladybugs crawling happily along leaves
Spectacular spring.

Finn Laidler (9)
Tollcross Primary School, Edinburgh

Spring Poem

Flaming foxes in morning sun
Awakening daffodils in warm sun
Season of the brightening

Baby warthogs playing in mud
Pigmy hippos having babies
Season of babies

Flowers escaping bulbs in sun
Cows grazing in warm sun
Season of life

Lion cubs playing on rocks
Crocs digging for their babies
Season of spring.

George Ewing (9)
Tollcross Primary School, Edinburgh

Winter

Squirrels digging desperately for nuts
Shivering animals
Melting moon

Noisy reindeer digging for grass
Crystal clear ice
Geese migrating

Clean snow
Ice as cold as a freezer
Frozen, frosty lakes

Children playing
Naked trees
Cold sun

Freezing fingers
Warm fires
Shivering spines.

Matias Edwin Gonzalez (9)
Tollcross Primary School, Edinburgh

The Season

Spring has sprung
Winter is done
Sunflowers bloom
Tall trees loom

Summer will shine
August, June, July
Birds won't leave a feather
Just enjoy the hot weather

Once again, winter has risen
The puddles are like a frosty prism
Everything is capped with snow
Kids think they hear, "Ho, ho, ho!"

Sam McCartan (9)
Tollcross Primary School, Edinburgh

Winter Becomes Spring

Crunchy snow
Old people say no
Cold water rippling
Silver geese flapping
Bloodshot moon
Never have prunes
Good old winter
Never disappear

Snow sheets disappear
The leaping deer
A beautiful grouse
As quiet as a mouse
Leaves slowly arise
Kingfishers dive
Daffodils bloom
There is no room.

Aaron Hedley (9)
Tollcross Primary School, Edinburgh

194

Spring

No coldness?
Birds chirping left and right
The sun is really hot
I am roasting, please help!

Snow disappears
Fields of really bright daffodils
Bluebells shining like diamonds
Daisies as white as snow

No storms
Just the sun, always out
Not any storms right now
It is really joyful today.

Rayyan Shafique (9)
Tollcross Primary School, Edinburgh

Season Poems

Is the cold over? Spring
Animals awakening from hibernation
Colourful flowers blooming
Icy sheets disappear

Life is coming!
Beautiful baby birds seeing light
Leaves growing back colourful
Bleating lambs

Is spring really here?
Flaming foxes in morning sun
Grass turning green again.

Kiayla Curry (9)
Tollcross Primary School, Edinburgh

Winter To Spring

Fog drifting in the air
Icy pearl moon
Cold wind blowing

Birds chirping
Icicles dropping
Frozen plants fall

Diving into spring
Flowers blooming
Sun rising above trees

Chicks chirping
Piglets squealing
Deer are cute.

Rubi Keles (8)
Tollcross Primary School, Edinburgh

Spring

Animals come home
Animal arrive
Newborn animals
Season of birth and life!

Leaves return to trees
Flowers blooming
Leaves come alive
Season of nature!

Birds sing in the distance
More light
More time
Season of light!

Maria Vilaro-Rojas (10)
Tollcross Primary School, Edinburgh

Spring

Winter's done, spring is delt
And snow will melt
Grass grows green
Lilypads float on clear lakes
Trees come back to life
Daffodils sprout up high
Frogs croaking on broken logs
Koi fish jump up rivers
Bears growl with happiness.

Georgio Adesanya (9)
Tollcross Primary School, Edinburgh

Winter

Winter awakening
Robins flying
Snow falling
Squirrels climbing
Kids building snowmen happily
Snow forming on roofs
Animals hibernating
Sparkling icy leaves
Dangling off trees
Birds hatching
Winter peacefulness.

Essa Lahoak (9)
Tollcross Primary School, Edinburgh

Spring

Deer walking in
The distance

Fluffy bunnies wander
For prey

Animals... hot
And sweaty

The heartwarming
Sun appears

The summer rises
The spring ends.

Steven Mccoag (9)
Tollcross Primary School, Edinburgh

Spring

Snow magically disappears
As well as darkness. A new life
Started, the eggs cracked of nests
Bears got out of their caves
Plants started growing again
Spring was the season of brightness.

Marc Armada (9)

Tollcross Primary School, Edinburgh

Winter

Melting sun
In the cloudy sky
Bitter cold air

Lovely sunset
Sad animals
They are cold
Bitter cold lakes

Snow weather
All foggy lakes
Bitter cold winter.

Scarlet Macdonald (9)
Tollcross Primary School, Edinburgh

Spring

Sun beaming
Flowers blooming
Bunnies hopping like kangaroos
Fox cubs play fighting
While mother fox rolls her eyes
Children playing
Birds singing...

Dean McMenigall (10)
Tollcross Primary School, Edinburgh

Spring

Blushing green grass
Birds chirping
Swinging trees
Buzzing bees
Insects wandering
The world blooming
Scorching sun.

Harris Gray (9)
Tollcross Primary School, Edinburgh

Breakfast

I can see Weetabix
I can hear bubbles pop
I can touch the Weetabix
I can taste the sweetness
I can feel crunches.

William Gallivan (11)
Two Rivers Primary School, Amington

Horses Trot

H airy
O ver the jump
R iding
S tables
E ating hay
S addle.

Elisha Wale (11)

Two Rivers Primary School, Amington

Sense Poem

I can see water
I can hear trouble
I can feel danger
I can taste soup
I can touch games.

Nate Ray (10)
Two Rivers Primary School, Amington

My Favourite Things

A haiku

I like Pokémon
And Brawl Stars as well
As Pokémon Go!

Archie Castagna (10)

Two Rivers Primary School, Amington

YOUNG WRITERS INFORMATION

We hope you have enjoyed reading this book – and that you will continue to in the coming years.

If you're a young writer who enjoys reading and creative writing, or the parent of an enthusiastic poet or story writer, do visit our website **www.youngwriters.co.uk**. Here you will find free competitions, workshops and games, as well as recommended reads, a poetry glossary and our blog. There's lots to keep budding writers motivated to write!

If you would like to order further copies of this book, or any of our other titles, then please give us a call or order via your online account.

Young Writers
Remus House
Coltsfoot Drive
Peterborough
PE2 9BF
(01733) 890066
info@youngwriters.co.uk

Join in the conversation!
Tips, news, giveaways and much more!

 YoungWritersUK    @YoungWritersCW